Deep Dive

First published by Allen & Unwin in 2017

Allen & Unwin
83 Alexander Street
Crows Nest NSW 2065
Australia
Phone: (61 2) 8425 0100
Email: info@allenandunwin.com
Web: www.allenandunwin.com

A Cataloguing-in-Publication entry is
available from the National Library of Australia
www.trove.nla.gov.au

ISBN 978 1 76029 602 5

For teaching resources, explore
www.allenandunwin.com/resources/for-teachers

Cover and text design by Sandra Nobes
Set in 16 pt ITC Stone Informal by Sandra Nobes
This book was printed in July 2017 at
McPherson's Printing Group, Australia.

1 3 5 7 9 10 8 6 4 2

macparkbooks.com

D-BOT SQUAD

BOOK 6
Deep Dive

MAC PARK

Illustrated by JAMES HART

ALLEN&UNWIN

SYDNEY • MELBOURNE • AUCKLAND • LONDON

Chapter One

Hunter, Charlie and Ethan were
on their d-bots deep under the
sea. And they were not alone.
Five massive kronosauruses
were swimming towards them.
Their mouths were open wide.

Ethan whispered into his
helmet's mic: 'Krons must go
up for air sometime.
I wish they'd do it now!'

'Me too,' Hunter agreed.
'But we can't wait for that.
Back up slowly, team.'

'Uh-oh,' Charlie said, looking
behind her. 'I think we're the
meat in the sandwich.'

Hunter and Ethan turned around. A school of giant squid was coming right at them.

'There are hundreds of them!' cried Ethan. 'Maybe a thousand! Some look as big as krons.'

Hunter looked from one group to the other. His mind filled with facts.

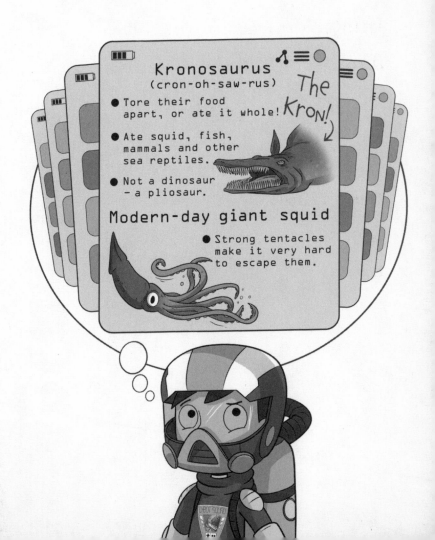

Kronosaurus
(cron-oh-saw-rus)

The Kron!

- Tore their food apart, or ate it whole!
- Ate squid, fish, mammals and other sea reptiles.
- Not a dinosaur – a pliosaur.

Modern-day giant squid

- Strong tentacles make it very hard to escape them.

'The krons will gobble up the squid,' Hunter said. 'It'll be a feeding frenzy. We have to get out of the way – fast!'

'And leave the squid to be eaten?' Charlie cried.

'Let's swim up a bit, then ray the krons,' Hunter said. 'With them gone, the squid will be safe.'

The team hit their remotes. Their d-bots rose upwards, just as the krons met the squid.

'Wooark! Wooark!'

Swish! Swish!

'We're too late. The krons are about to attack!' said Charlie.

Wooooosh! Wooooosh!

Schwoo! Schwoo!

'The giant squid are squirting
ink into the water,' said Ethan.

'Our torches are useless now.
I can't see anything through
this ink,' Charlie said.

'Keep going up!' Hunter shouted.
He splashed out of the water
and spied an island nearby.
It was the island where he'd
caught his first dinosaur – the
pterodactyl!

'Charlie! Ethan!' he yelled. But
Hunter was alone.

Chapter Two

'**Aaargh!**' Hunter heard Ethan cry through his speakers. 'I'm wrapped in squid tentacles.'

Hunter plunged back into the water. 'Hang on, I'm coming! Charlie?'

'I'm okay,' Charlie said, 'but I'm trapped too. Don't come back, Hunter. The squid will trap you as well.'

'I'll be careful,' said Hunter. 'And don't worry. Nothing can get through our suits.'

'I hope you're right,' Ethan said.

Hunter moved slowly downwards.
He heard the sea battle, but he
could only see blackness.

'Wooark! **Wooark!**'

Wooooosh!

'Wooark! **Wooark!**'

Crash! Hunter landed on the tail of Ethan's d-bot. The krons were deeper down, feeding on other squid.

'I think we should teleport out and come back again,' Ethan said.

'No. No teleporting,' Charlie
said firmly. 'The giant squid
we're touching would come
with us. And they would die
out of the water. We can't let
that happen.'

Hunter frowned. 'But I can't
leave you tangled up like this.
I say we—'

'Wait!' Charlie broke in.

'We wait! This is how squid catch their food. They'll soon work out we aren't fish. Then they'll let us go.'

So they waited, as the battle raged on below.

'**Wooark! Wooark!**'

Wooooosh!

'Wooark! Wooark!'

Wooooosh!

'All those poor squid,' said Hunter. 'If these ones would let you two go, we could save the others!'

'Keep as still as you can, Ethan,' said Charlie. 'That will help.'

Little by little, the ink cleared.

At last, the squid let go of
Charlie and Ethan. Then the
squid glided through the water,
away from danger.

'Finally!' Ethan said.

'Good thinking, Charlie,' Hunter said. 'Now, let's go deeper and find those five krons.'

The team swam downwards.

'There are so few squid left,' Charlie said sadly. 'They've all been eaten.'

'And where are the krons?' Hunter asked.

'Hunting for more food, I'll bet,' said Charlie. 'Krons moved in packs, so at least they'll be together.'

'We need to find them before they find food,' said Ethan.

'Let's look around down here first,' Hunter said.

The team dived deeper still, to the ocean floor.

'Look! An underwater cave,' Charlie said. She shone her torch inside. 'It's massive, and it has tunnels.'

'Are the krons in there?' Ethan asked.

'I can't see them,' Charlie said. She went into the cave. 'It's a big cave, but the tunnels are narrow. One tunnel is really long. I can see a hole at the end.'

Charlie swam back out to Hunter and Ethan. 'Cool cave, but no krons,' she said.

Hunter nodded. 'Never mind. Let's go to the surface. They may have gone up for air.'

'And then let's split up,' Ethan added. 'There's a lot of ocean to cover.'

They reached the surface. There was no sign of the krons.

Charlie flew away from the island, over deeper and deeper ocean.

Smart, thought Hunter. *Krons like deep water.*

Ethan turned his d-bot right. Hunter turned his left.

Soon after, Ethan cried, 'I found them!'

'And I've found a pod of killer whales,' said Charlie. 'They're heading towards Ethan.'

Hunter and Ethan sped towards Charlie. They could see the whales moving in the water. There were so many of them.

'What are we going to do?' said Ethan.

Hunter's mind worked quickly.

Modern-day killer whales

- Almost as long as a school bus.
- Hunt in deadly pods.
- Eat much the same food as the krons.
- Mammals — and krons ate mammals!

But who would win the battle, the whales or the krons? We don't want to find out!

'This will be worse than the squid battle,' Hunter said. 'We need a plan. A plan to keep the whales and krons apart.'

'We need to think fast,' said Charlie. 'The whales are speeding up. They must somehow know the krons are there!'

Chapter Three

Hunter thought and thought.

Can we get the five krons into that underwater cave? he wondered.

'Hunter, the cave!' Charlie cried, like a mind-reader. 'If we got them into it, they'd be safe.'

'But how could we ray the krons from above in there?' Hunter asked.

Charlie shook her head. 'Not the krons – we want the killer whales in the cave!'

Hunter blinked. *Of course!* he thought. A plan began to take shape in his mind.

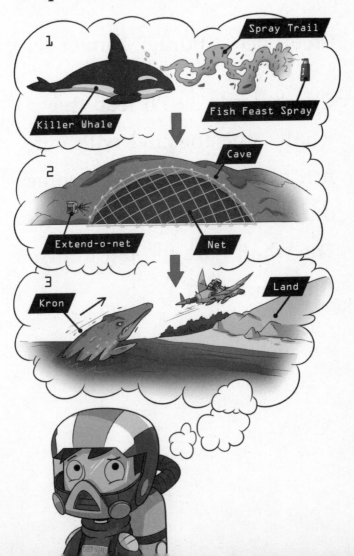

'Great idea, Charlie!' Hunter said.

Charlie smiled. 'I'll lead the whales into the cave with our fish feast spray. Then I'll come out that hole on the other side. The whales are too big to fit through it.'

Hunter turned to Ethan. 'Next you block the entrance to the cave with the extend-o-net.'

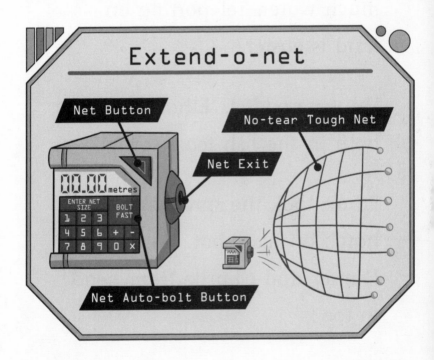

Extend-o-net

Net Button

No-tear Tough Net

Net Exit

00.00 metres

ENTER NET SIZE

BOLT FAST

1 2 3

4 5 6 + -

7 8 9 0 ×

Net Auto-bolt Button

'Okay. And you lure the krons to the island,' Ethan said. 'Our rays can't get through too much water. Teleporting on land is easier.'

Hunter nodded. 'Ethan, cover us both in the fish feast spray!'

Ethan took the spray from a hatch on his d-bot. He sprayed Hunter and Charlie from head to toe.

'**Urrrgh! Gross!**' said Ethan.

Hunter groaned and took the spray from Ethan. 'I'm covered in rotten fish.'

Charlie wrinkled her nose. 'It stinks, even through our helmets. The whales will totally follow me.'

'Okay,' said Ethan. 'You're ready. Let's do it!' He and Charlie flew into the sea, towards the whales.

Hunter flew towards the krons.

Then he dived into the water.

'Come on, krons,' he said. 'Your
turn for food.'

He whirled in the water. Hunks
of rotten fish flew from his suit.
The krons came towards him.

'Good krons!' he said. 'You can
smell me, can't you?'

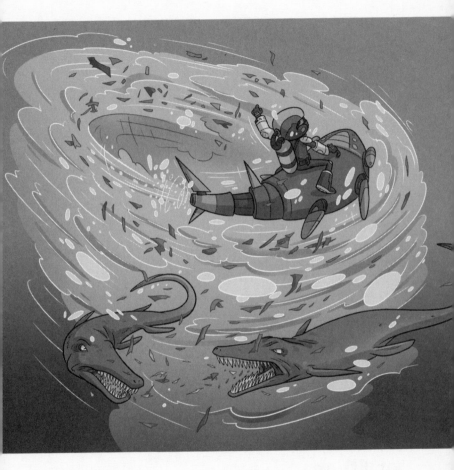

Then Hunter sped towards the
island. The krons sped after him.

'Charlie has the whales in the cave,' said Ethan. 'And the net is in place.'

'Good,' said Hunter. 'The krons are at the island. I've sprayed the sand with fish feast! I'm on my way back now.'

Hunter reached the cave. But there was no sign of Charlie or Ethan.

Chapter Four

'Charlie, Ethan, where are you?' Hunter called.

Brrrr! Brrrr!

'**Arrgh!**' Hunter cried. 'What's that noise? What's going on?'

'We need help!' Ethan shouted.
'Charlie's stuck in the cave with
the killer whales. The hole
wasn't as big as she thought.'

Hunter sped above the cave to
its other end. Ethan was trying
to make the hole bigger. He
was drilling into the rock from
the outside.

'Give me your hand!' Hunter cried to Charlie. 'I'll pull you through the hole.'

'What about my d-bot?' Charlie cried. 'I can't leave Legend. Just a bit more drilling and we'll both be free.'

Hunter began to drill too. *She named her d-bot!* he thought.

A killer whale was closing in on Charlie. Its mouth was wide open.

'Quick!' Ethan cried.

'Almost … almost … phew!' Charlie shouted. She darted through the hole.

The whale's mouth closed, gulping only water. Its nose was stuck in the hole.

'Are you okay?' Ethan asked
Charlie.

Hunter frowned. *I should have
asked that*, he thought. 'Let's go,'
he said instead. 'We have
a job to do.'

The team raced to the cave's entrance. They took off the extend-o-net, so the whales could get out. Then they shot upwards at full speed. They flew from the water towards the island.

'I hope those krons are still where I left them,' Hunter said.

Near the island, the team saw five heads pop out from the sea.

'There they are!' Ethan called. 'Now let's get them up onto the sand and ray them.'

'I'll lead them to the shore with more fish feast,' said Charlie.

'Okay,' said Hunter. 'But don't
get too close. They really love
that stuff!' He handed her the
spray.

'I'll be careful,' said Charlie. 'Get
ready for when they surface.'

'We'll be here,' said Ethan.

Charlie smiled. Then she and
her d-bot dived into the sea.

The five krons landed on the beach, in a pile.

'Quick!' Charlie called, flying into the air. 'It's now or never.'

But Hunter's and Ethan's blades were now stuck in seaweed.

'Set your jets to go the other way, Ethan,' Hunter cried.

Vwaar! Vwaar!

The jet blades turned and turned the other way. The seaweed started to shift. But Ethan and Hunter weren't free yet.

'Faster, Hunter!' Ethan cried. 'Or we'll miss our chance to teleport the krons!'

Chapter Five

The beached krons were starting
to move. Hunter's and Ethan's
blades broke free of the
seaweed at last. They both
zoomed towards Charlie.

'Okay, let's do this!' Hunter called.

'I'm good to go,' Ethan said.

Charlie took control. 'On my count of three. **One, two...**'

'Three!' the team shouted.

Three rays hit the one big pile of krons. The krons vanished.

The team landed their d-bots
and sat on the soft white sand.
Hunter was deep in thought.

Hunter smiled. He felt good.
I'm part of an awesome team, he
thought. *And no one makes fun
of me.*

Crackle! Crunch! Snap!

Charlie jumped up. 'Did you
hear that?' she whispered.

Tap! Scratch! Tap!

Hunter listened. 'Yes! What is
that?'

Ethan pointed to a mound of shells. 'It's coming from over there!'

Hunter looked around. 'This is exactly where I caught my first dino,' he said. 'And it was picking at that same mound.'

'Oh!' Charlie shouted. 'Something in that mound is moving.'

The team rushed over.

'It's a dino-nest!' Hunter cried.
'Look, eggs! The pterodactyl
I caught laid eggs.'

'But the eggs all look different,'
said Charlie. 'They can't all be
ptero eggs.'

Crack! 'Screech!' **Crack!**

'Whatever they are,' said Ethan,
'they're hatching!'

Hunter peered into a hatching
egg. A baby pterodactyl bit his
nose. 'Ouch!' he cried.

Hunter picked up the baby
ptero. 'You're totally awesome!'
he said. 'Perfect in every way.'

'More eggs are starting to hatch,'
Ethan said. 'We have to get
them back to base. We have to
show Ms Stegg.'

The team gently picked up the
eggs. They put them in their
d-bots' hatches. Then they
jumped onto their d-bots and
teleported to D-Bot Squad base.

Chapter Six

Back at base, Ms Stegg and the team couldn't believe their eyes. The eggs were on a tray, and they were all hatching!

Crack! 'Screech!' **Crack!**

'That's a baby triceratops!'
Charlie gasped.

Crack! 'Screech!' **Crack!**

'And look,' cried Hunter,
'another one's hatching. It's a
little raptor foot!'

'Check out that last egg,' said
Ethan. 'I wonder what it's going
to be.'

Crack! 'Screech!' **Crack!**

Everyone's eyes almost popped
from their heads.

'A T-rex!' gasped Ms Stegg.

'How did the ptero have all these different eggs?' wondered Hunter.

'And are there any more eggs out there?' Ms Stegg pushed some buttons on her d-band.

'And look at the baby ptero,' said Ethan. 'It's really big already.'

'The raptor is growing fast too!' Charlie said.

The little dinosaurs kept
growing – faster and faster,
bigger and bigger.

'Ms Stegg, how can they grow so
quickly?' Ethan asked.

'I'm not sure. But I don't like
the look of it,' said Ms Stegg.
'We need to stop their growth.'

The dino-tray had a switch on its side. Ms Stegg pressed it. Rays shot out from all around the edges. All the baby dinosaurs were caught in a ray-bubble.

The dinosaurs stopped moving. It was like they were frozen in time.

'It looks like teleporting!' said
Ethan.

'Yes,' said Ms Stegg. 'But they're
not going anywhere. This ray
stops them growing.'

'Are they safe in there?' asked
Charlie.

'Of course,' Ms Stegg said.

'Wow! For how long?' asked
Hunter. 'And what will we—'

Bip! Bip! Bip! Bip!
Bip! Bip! Bip! Bip!

'What's that?' asked Charlie.

Ms Stegg went to some screens
on the wall.

'I used my d-band to send
drone-cams to the island,' she
said. 'I wanted to see if there
were more eggs there. The bips
are the drone-cam alerts.'

'So many bips!' said Hunter. He covered his ears.

Ms Stegg pressed lots of buttons very quickly. 'Stay calm, everyone,' she said. But it wasn't easy to stay calm.

'What's going on?' cried Ethan over the noise.

'There are more dino-eggs on the island,' said Ms Stegg. 'And who knows where else.'

'How did this happen?' shouted Charlie.

Ms Stegg took a step back. 'I'm not sure yet,' she said. She was frowning. 'But I'm afraid more eggs have hatched. A lot more. And now all those dinosaurs are on the loose!'

Will D-Bot Squad

crack under stress?

Read Book 7, *Mega Hatch,*

to find out!

Join

D-BOT SQUAD

Catch all 8 books!

MAC PARK

macparkbooks.com